PIPPA PARVIN
AND THE
MYSTERY OF THE
RUINED
CORRIDOR

PIPPA PARVIN

AND THE

MYSTERY OF THE

RUINED

CORRIDOR

BOOK 1

Printed in the United States of America

First Printing, 2020

ISBN: 978-1-7339154-9-6

WorkHorse Productions, Inc.

Formatting by:

emtippettsbookdesigns.com

OTHER LITTLE BOOKS OF **BIG** CHOICES

Billy the Chimera Hunter

Billy Chan and the Case of the Pengurtles
Billy Chan and the Little Lost Orcoose
Billy Chan and the Fronine Invasion
Billy Chan and the Walrar Bear Abduction
Billy Chan Goes Where the Sheelephants Roam
Billy Chan Chases a Burkey through Albuquerque
Billy Chan Rescues a Moark Named Mark
Billy Chan and the Stinky Goatopus
Billy Chan Goes to the World of the Felidavians
Billy Chan and the Clash of the Bungolins
Billy Chan and Operation Bager
Billy Chan and the Giraffigator Showdown

Pippa the Werefox

Pippa Parvin and the Mystery of the Ruined Corridor
Pippa Parvin and the Mystery of the Missing Pencil
Pippa Parvin and the Mystery of the Unidentified Flying Object
Pippa Parvin and the Mystery of the Fork in the Garden
Pippa Parvin and the Mystery of the Stolen Lunches
Pippa Parvin and the Mystery of the Missing Wellies

THE RUINED CORRIDOR

"**P**ippa!" Aunt Vivian calls up the stairs. "Come on downstairs."

You stand in the front hallway of a strange, cramped little house. It's a gray day outside, but the land around is green and lush and goes on for miles. You've never been this far from the city before.

The front hallway you stand in has a

row of hooks high on the wall where several coats hang. The walls were once white, but are yellowed and scuffed with age. Still, it's a nice house. It feels warm and cozy, like a home.

Pippa comes down the stairs. She's got pale white skin, freckles, and bright red hair that is tied up with a bow. At the sight of you, she smiles as if you are a long-lost friend, even though you've never met each other before.

"This is your cousin, Pippa Parvin," Aunt Vivian tells you.

"We're so glad we found you," cries Pippa, running forward to grasp your hands. "I didn't even know I had a cousin."

You didn't know this either. You've been an orphan for as long as you can remember. It wasn't until your foster home got a letter that you learned your father had a little sister who lives out in the country with her daughter. Now here you are, in their home.

It's hard to smile, but you do your best. It is good to have family, you think. You've never had one before.

There's something about this house and the way it smells, though. It's as if they have a dog, but you see no dog. You see no fur on the floor nor leash hung up with the coats. There is no water bowl, and there are footprints in the carpet. None of them are pawprints. And yet...

A thrill goes through you.

"Come upstairs," says Pippa. "I'll show you your room."

You follow your cousin up the narrow stairs to a landing. She points to the bedroom on the left. "That is yours."

Through the door is the biggest bedroom you've ever had. It has a sloped ceiling and a bed tucked into the corner. Against the wall is a giant shelf of books.

"Have you any things?" Pippa asks. "Any clothes? Any toys?"

You hold out the small bag you've got with you. It's full of clothes: three shirts and some trousers. These, and what you are wearing, are all you have. At least your shoes are nice and new.

Pippa frowns, then goes across the hall. A moment later she returns, carrying a stuffed fox. "Here," she says. "He is yours. He doesn't have a name. You must think of one."

A gift? For you? You blink back tears as you take the stuffed fox from your cousin. He has ruddy red fur and black plastic eyes. You hug him tight to your chest. You wonder, is it a sign?

"Once you've seen your room," Aunt Vivian calls up the stairs, "come down and we'll

4

visit your school."

"Mum works at the school," Pippa explains. "She's got a key. Come on. Let us show you around."

The school is very different than the one you went to in the city. That one didn't have these big iron gates or a play yard out front. It just had a front door with the name of the school carved in stone beside it. This new school sits by itself, away from the village.

Aunt Vivian unlocks the gate, and you follow her and Pippa across the play yard to the main door, which Aunt Vivian also unlocks.

"Oh no," she says, as she steps inside. "What happened here?"

Pippa pushes her way in and pulls you after her.

You find yourself in a long corridor

littered with paper. Up on one wall is a row of paintings, probably made by an art class, but several of them have been torn down and shredded. Bits and pieces of them are scattered all over. Splotches of paint also dot the floor and the walls. The corridor is ruined.

"This is my class," says Pippa, pointing at the paintings. "Who would do this?"

"It doesn't matter, Pippa," says Aunt Vivian. "I'll tape the paintings back together and they'll be as good as new."

Your cousin doesn't seem happy with this, but leads you down the corridor to another classroom. "This will be your classroom," she says.

It's a tidy little room with lots of bright colors in the carpet and on the walls. It's as if the room is one big, warm hug. It's nothing like your plain and dingy classroom back in

London.

Aunt Vivian repairs the paintings and cleans up the corridor while Pippa shows you around the school and play yard. Even though she's too big for the slide and the swings on this side of the school, she plays with you, pushing you in the swings and catching you as you go down the slide.

You've decided it's good to have a cousin.

Once Aunt Vivian finishes cleaning the corridor, she locks up the school and the three of you walk home.

"Psst!" Pippa's voice wakes you from a deep sleep. It's so *quiet* out in the country. There's no sound of traffic or people.

You peel one eye open and look at your cousin. Her face looks very pale in the dimness.

7

"Do you like your stuffy?" she asks, pointing to the fox you have hugged to your chest.

"Yes," you say.

"Does it mean anything... special, to you?" she asks.

You don't know whether to be scared or excited. Pippa knows! She knows your secret.

"Right," she says. "I'll go first." She goes to the middle of the room and her outline blurs. She shifts from a girl into a fox with dainty paws and a pointed nose.

Your heart beats so fast you can hear it thundering away. You throw off your covers, get out of bed, and shut your eyes. You feel your body flow and change and then you are also a fox, with your own dainty paws. You're a smaller fox than Pippa. You are only a little cub and Pippa is a bigger cub with longer legs and a longer tail.

Pippa jumps up and down in excitement, then shifts back to human form. "You're like me!" she whispers.

You shift back as well. "Is everyone in the family a werefox?" you ask. You had always thought you were the only one.

"I don't know," she says. "I though *I* was the only one! I want to go investigate the mystery of the ruined corridor. Will you join me?" She says those last words very seriously, like an adult.

"Investigate?" you say.

"Yes. I've got Mum's keys. Put on your shoes and follow me." She pushes open your window and climbs out. "This used to be my room," she says, poking her head back in. "So I know this works."

You're quite a bit smaller than Pippa, so

you have to climb the bookcase to get to the window. It's easy for you to slip out, though, into the chill night air. The moon is full, giving off silvery light, and a nightbird sings somewhere in the distance.

Pippa shimmies down the roof and drops to the ground.

You do your best to keep up and then you are both running through the forest towards the school. It isn't far. Rather than unlock the gate, Pippa has you shift to fox form, slip through the bars, and then hands you the keys. A moment later she goes into fox form and follows you. The two of you scamper across the play yard and Pippa shifts back to a girl at the front door.

"So you stay a fox," she whispers to you. "It's easier to investigate if one of us is a fox." She unlocks the door and pushes it open.

You slip inside. It's dark, but as a fox, you

can see very well in the dark. The world looks gray, but it's easy to see the pieces of tape where the paintings were hung earlier that day.

"Right," says Pippa, shutting the door behind her. "I think there are two places we should investigate. My classroom and the art room. Where do you want to go first?"

Her classroom (turn to page 14)

The art room (turn to page 20)

RETURN TO THE CLASSROOM

You think you may have missed a clue in the classroom, so you dart back in there and hop up onto the desks. Where were the two places you could look in here?

Oh yes! Pippa wanted you to look at the windows, where someone might have come in, and at the paintings Aunt Vivian repaired. Which do you want to check for clues?

Go check the windows (turn to page 38).

Go look at the repaired paintings (turn to page 33).

IN THE CLASSROOM

You head into the classroom. In fox form, all you can see are the bottoms of the desks and chairs. There is gum stuck under one of the desks that you can see.

You hop up on a chair and then up on top of a desk to get a better look around. Everyone has their name written neatly on cards taped to their desks, and the cards are decorated with pictures. The desk you're standing on says, "Simon" and is decorated with rubber-stamped leaves.

Pippa walks around the room, searching with her human eyes while you hop from desk to desk. There are nine desks in all. They belong to: Millie (decorated with frogs jumping on a duck), Bastian (decorated with birds), Nick (decorated with tulips), Kiran (decorated with ducks), Wendy (decorated with bees), Thomas (decorated with frogs), and Robert (decorated with ducks crossed out). The ninth desk is Pippa's, and she decorated her card with foxes. You already know how you will decorate your card if you get one.

You sniff all the desks and smell a lot of things, but it's hard for you to tell the smells apart. You can make out the smell of the hand lotion your teacher at your old school used, but it smells like a lot of the students use it too.

You leap onto the teacher's desk and find a big bottle of the lotion, turned to face the classroom. It looks like anyone who wants to use it, can. This teacher seems a lot nicer than the teacher you had at your old school.

Pippa, meanwhile, is walking around the edge of the classroom, staying out of your way.

She comes by the teacher's desk and says, "This is the only classroom with windows that face the woods and not the village." She points at the windows on the far wall. "This would be a good place for someone who wanted to sneak into the classroom to come in, but they're too high for me to reach easily. I would need to stand on a chair. Perhaps you could jump up and look to see if all the windows are locked?"

You look up at the windows. There is a shelf that looks sturdy enough to hold a fox. If you jumped up onto the radiator, then onto the shelf, you could jump up to the windows.

"Or," says Pippa, "we can look at the pictures Mum taped together."

You know you will need to look in both of those places. Where would you like to look first?

Up on the windowsill (turn to page 38)

At the pictures Aunt Vivian has repaired (turn to page 33)

To the art room, if you haven't been there yet (turn to page 20)

If you've already been to the art room but want to return, turn to page 18.

RETURN TO THE ART ROOM

Y ou feel like you may have missed something in the art room, so you run back there and jump up on a chair, then onto the table. There were two places to look for clues. One was in the pigeonholes, to find out who wasn't supposed to be using orange paint. The other was the back door, where the footprints lead. Which place do you want to look?

Look in the pigeonholes (turn to page 29).

Look at the back door (turn to page 23).

THE ART ROOM

You remember where the art room is. Pippa showed you this morning.

You head there, with your cousin following along behind. This room is filled with moonlight, meaning even Pippa can see everything in here. You can see better though, as a fox.

Since you only walked past this room

earlier, this is your first chance to get a good look. There is a high table with chairs all around it and a chalkboard on the far wall. The teacher's desk is in the corner.

"All of the orange paint is dumped out," says Pippa, looking at the jars of paint on the shelf. "For those paintings that were hung in the corridor, we had to paint without one color. Half of us couldn't use orange, and the other half of us couldn't use green. This person must have been in the no-orange group. We all have pigeonholes. I can look through those to see the teacher's notes about who was in which group." She points to a shelf on the far wall with little dividers. Students' names are taped above each pigeonhole. Your American friend at your old school called these "cubbyholes." They are much smaller than what you would call a cubbyhole, though. They only fit a few papers and a small pot of paint.

You, however, keep looking around and spy a line of footprints, outlined in orange paint, leading to the back door. It looks like that is how whoever tore up the paintings got out of the school.

Pippa notices these, too. "Maybe we should clean this up," she says. "Once we've gathered all the clues. Poor Miss Anne won't want to have to deal with this."

Where do you want to look?

In the pigeonholes (turn to page 29)

At the back door (turn to page 23)

In the classroom, if you haven't been there already (turn to page 14)

If you have been to the classroom but not yet gotten both clues from there, turn to page 12.

THE BACK DOOR

You walk across the table and drop down at the far end, near to the back door. First you examine the shoe prints, as they seem like an obvious clue.

Pippa squats down beside you and takes a good look. "If I was a police detective, I would be able to figure out what size these are and what type of shoe it is. I'm not, though. You

23

don't happen to know the different types of shoe prints?"

You droop your head and tail, knowing that she'll take that as a "No." How would a person learn about different kinds of shoe prints anyhow?

"I can't even tell if these belong to a boy or a girl," says Pippa. "So they are no help."

She gets up and goes to look at the back door, which has smudges of orange paint on the doorknob.

"If only I knew how to collect fingerprints!" she says.

This would solve the case at once, you know. This also means that if anyone at the school calls the police, they will be able to figure out who committed the crime. All you can tell from the footprints and fingerprints is that it is someone roughly Pippa's age and size.

"Hang on." Pippa peers at the keyhole. "Someone's jammed something in here." She leans in, staring hard. "Whoever wants to unlock this door won't be able to. I'm going to get some tweezers." She goes out into the hallway, leaving you alone in the art room.

You curl into a little ball, waiting for her to come back.

Pippa returns a moment later with a pair of tweezers and a tissue in her hand.

"I hope this doesn't make too much of a mess," she says, carefully prying at something with the tweezers.

Whatever it is, doesn't come out all in one chunk, it stretches and stretches. Pippa wipes the tweezers on the tissue and then pokes them in the keyhole again to get more of the stretchy stuff.

"It's gum," she says.

She works very carefully, pulling the gum out of the lock as best she can.

"I'm not sure I've got it all," she says, putting her eye to the keyhole again. "But I've got as much of it as I can."

She bends down and holds out the tissue to you. "Chewing gum," she says.

You sniff the gum and smell the scent of milkshake. That's a very unusual scent for gum!

You look and see that there is gum on the bottom of the table, but none of it smells like a milkshake.

You don't know if people always sit in the same place at the table anyhow. There's only one room you know of that has assigned seating.

You head to the classroom and there find all of the desks set out in rows. On the bottom of some of them is gum, and when you go closer to sniff, you find that some of the gum smells like a milkshake. Pippa follows you and when she sees you point at a desk, she reads off the name from the name card on top of the desk.

"Simon," she reads. "Millie, and Kiran. Right, then. This is a clue."

She scoops you up and takes you back to the art room, placing you on the table. She throws the gum in the bin. "So it's one of those three," she says. "Where do you want to look next?"

You have found a clue: the chewing gum. The gum in the keyhole was a very unusual flavor only some of the students chew. You need to collect four clues to solve this mystery. If you don't have them all yet, you can...

...look at the pigeonholes (turn to page 29).

...look in the classroom, if you haven't been there yet (turn to page 14).

If you have been in the classroom but not gotten both of the clues there, turn to page 12.

Think you have all four clues? Turn to page 45.

IN THE PIGEONHOLES

The pigeonholes are each a small space where students can store their things. You jump down from the table and go towards the pigeonholes. Once you reach them, you sit down and neatly wrap your tail around your feet.

"Pigeonholes it is!" says Pippa. She leans down and reaches into the first one. She holds the paper up so that she can read it by moonlight. "Millie was not to use any orange," she says.

She goes to the next one. "Simon wasn't to use any green."

In the next one is a note that says, "Bastian was not to use any orange."

"Robert was not to use any orange."

"Nick was not to use any green."

"Wendy was not to use any green."

"Thomas was not to use any green."

"Kiran was not to use any orange."

Pippa comes to the last pigeonhole. "This is mine. I was not to use any orange. I use a lot of orange because I paint a lot of foxes. The art teacher wanted me to paint anything but a fox."

She looks down at you. "Well, we've got four people who weren't supposed to use any orange. I suppose the person who destroyed the paintings was one of those four? Where shall we look now?"

You leap back up onto a chair and onto the table so that you can look around and decide where to go next.

You've found a clue: the orange paint. Four students were not allowed to paint in orange for the assignment. You need four clues to solve this mystery. If you don't yet have all four, you can look...

...at the back door (turn to page 23)

...in the classroom, if you haven't looked there already (turn to page 14)

If you've been to the classroom, but not

gotten both clues from there, turn to page 12.

Think you have all four clues? Turn to page 45.

THE PAINTINGS

The repaired paintings are laid out on a table near the door, and you head for it. You're able to hop onto a chair and then onto the table where the damaged paintings are spread out, neatly repaired with cellotape.

"We had to paint animals," says Pippa. "Oh... I reckon I see a theme here."

All of the torn up paintings are of ducks.

Three paintings in all.

You know who hates ducks!

Pippa runs after you and catches up as you land on Robert's desk. You point to his name card with your paw.

It takes Pippa a moment to focus on it in the dim light. "Oh, of course!" she says. "On the first day of school we were supposed to decorate our cards with our favorite things! Though they had to be things the teacher had a stamp for." She laughs. "I forget what Robert's favorite thing was, but there was no stamp for it, so he said anything but ducks and drew lines through a bunch of ducks."

You hop from desk to desk to find everyone who put ducks on their cards; you find two more people: Kiran, and Millie. Millie also doesn't seem to like ducks; she has frogs jumping on ducks. Kiran just has ducks. No lines. No frogs hopping on them.

Pippa notes these three names. "But did the person who tore up the paintings like ducks or hate them? I suppose it's odd for someone who likes ducks to tear up pictures of ducks?"

She goes back to the table to look at the paintings again. "The paintings that got torn up are by Bastian, Simon, and Kiran. It'd be sad if someone tore up their own painting."

You go back to the table, landing on it with light paws. Two of the paintings are of common, brown ducks, but one is very different looking. Its feathers are drawn with black ink and filled in with bright colors: blue and green and yellow and red. If it wasn't in water, you wouldn't know it was a duck. You've never seen such a colorful one before. In the lower corner, Kiran has signed his name.

"Right," says Pippa, "we should keep

looking. Where should we go next?"

You have found a clue: the duck connection. The person tore up only pictures of ducks. You need four clues to solve this mystery. If you don't yet have all four, you can keep looking.

You can...

...go look on the windowsill (turn to page 38)

...go to the art room, if you haven't been there already (turn to page 20)

or if you've already been to the art room

but not looked everywhere, turn to page 18.

Think you have all four clues? Turn to page 45.

ON THE WINDOWSILL

You head for the wall where the windows are. Pippa follows you and catches you when you try to jump onto the radiator, but slide off. It's more slippery than it looks.

Your cousin's hands are gentle and she hugs you to her chest. "Be careful," she says. "I can lift you up."

You've never let anyone carry you in fox

form, before, but it does make it much easier. She reaches up and puts you on the shelf, which is full of odds and ends like seashells, pretty bottles, and a candle that reeks of vanilla.

The windowsill is a short hop up from the shelf and you make it easily, balance for a moment, and then start examining the windows. Outside is deep, velvety night. Something rustling below tells you there are probably some garbage bins under the windows, and some animal is going through them, looking for a snack.

With your paw, you press on the window, then look around at the window frame to find the latch. This first window is shut and locked tight, so you move onto the second one, which is also locked.

On you go until you reach the one at the far end. This one isn't closed all the way. The latch has slipped a bit. You push against the window with your paw, but you aren't strong enough as a fox to open the window.

So you turn around and yip to your cousin, hopping up and down so that she knows which window to look at.

"All right, hang on," she says.

She gets a chair and moves it to right under your perch, then climbs up on top of it and looks at the window, her red hair bright, even in the dim moonlight. With the palm of her hand, she pushes on the window and it opens, but not far.

"Can you see outside?" she asks. "Is there anything anyone could stand on out there?"

You peer through the now open window. Sure enough, directly below is a garbage bin. Next to it is a plastic box that someone set out to use as a stair. Someone could easily climb up this and come through the window.

You yip and hop, hoping Pippa understands that means "Yes."

"All right," she says. "This is where they must have got in or out or both. Look and sniff around the window frame and see if you find anything."

You carefully trace your nose around the edge of the frame, but the smells don't mean much to you. Something tickles your nose and you sneeze.

Pippa reaches out and snatches something from the air in front of your face.

"It's a hair," she says. She takes it over to the teacher's desk, switches on the lamp, and holds the hair up to the light. "It's a brown hair," she says. "I don't suppose you can sniff it and match it to a scent on one of the desks?" She brings it back over to you.

You give the hair a good sniff, but it mostly smells like Pippa. You droop your head and tail, and hope she understands that means, "No."

"I've got an old journal," she says. "Mum never told me whose it was, but there's a whole bit on learning to hunt by smell. We'll need to read it, I think. But at least we know that whoever did this has brown hair. This hair is so short, it could be a boy or a girl.

She holds out her arms to you and you hop into them and let her lower you to the floor.

"Right," she says, walking to the doorway, where the class picture hangs. She lifts you up so that you can see the faces of the class. There's enough light from the lamp that you can see everyone's hair color.

"Millie, Kiran, Bastian, and Simon all have brown hair," she says, pointing. "So it's probably one of those four. Where shall we go next?"

You found a clue: the strand of hair. The person who tore up the paintings has brown hair. You will need four clues to solve this mystery. Where do you want to look next?

At the repaired paintings (turn to page 33)

In the art room for the first time (turn to page 20)

If you've already been to the art room

but not gotten both clues from there, turn to page 18.

Think you have all four clues? Turn to page 45.

THE FOUR CLUES

You should have four clues. If you don't have all four, below are the page numbers for any clues you have missed. The four places to get clues are:

On the windowsill (on page 38)

In the paintings (on page 33)

In the back door (on page 23)

In the pigeonholes (on page 29)

If you've got all four clues, then it's time
to piece them together. Go on to the next page.

DEDUCTIONS

"Now it's time to make deductions!" says Pippa. She goes to her desk in the classroom and you follow, shifting back into human form as you do.

"What are de-duc-tions?" you ask, sounding out the word carefully.

"When you figure out what the clues

say," says Pippa, "you are making deductions. Let's look at the clues."

She gets out a sheet of paper and a pencil from her desk and uses the light on the teacher's desk, which is small. Nobody outside should see it.

"First," she says, "is the strand of hair." She writes down the names of everyone with brown hair:

Millie, Kiran, Bastian, Simon

"Next is the gum," she says. She writes down the names of everyone who chews the strange flavor of gum:

Simon, Millie, Kiran

"Then there's the orange paint," she says. "Here are the people who couldn't use orange that day." She writes the following names:

Kiran, Millie, Bastian, Robert

"Then we consider the paintings that were torn up. Either the person doesn't like ducks, or they felt strongly about ducks, so I'm writing down both the people who hate ducks, and the person who likes them." She writes:

Robert, Kiran, Millie

"Right, I think we should start with the duck-haters," she says. "That's who's most likely to tear up a duck painting, right? Not liking ducks would be the *motive*, or the reason why someone did what they did. Robert hates ducks, but he doesn't have brown hair and doesn't chew the right kind of gum. So we deduce..."

She looks at me to make sure I catch that word.

"We *deduce*," she repeats, "that it is not Robert. That's a deduction. Millie hates ducks, has brown hair, chews the right kind of gum, and wasn't allowed to use orange that day. Also, hers wasn't one of the paintings torn up." Pippa taps her pencil on Millie's name. "Kiran, though, he also has brown hair, chews the right kind of gum, and wasn't allowed to use orange paint. He loves ducks and his own painting was torn up."

"So we know who it is, right?" I ask.

"Can you deduce who it is?" Pippa asks me.

Can you guess who tore up the paintings?

Make your best guess and then turn to the next page.

THE CULPRIT

"I know who did it," says Pippa, "and now I feel sad."

"Why?" you ask.

Pippa goes back to the paintings and picks up Kiran's. "He spent ages on this, you know. Worked really hard. Even went in during lunch to finish it up, and everyone teased him for it. They thought it was such an odd way to paint a duck."

"You think they made him mad?"

"Maybe," says Pippa. "I think made him sad. I also think he's also the only person who would get upset about not being allowed to use a color. The rest of us didn't mind, but he wanted as many colors as possible."

"Oh..." you say. "I've never met anyone named Kiran." You're ashamed to admit this.

"Well, right, it's an Indian name. Kiran's also the only person in our class whose family is from India. The thing about him being from India..."

She goes over to the computer and taps the keyboard to wake it up. Then she types in an internet search and shows me the screen.

It is full of pictures with dark outlines and bright colors.

"It's an Indian style of painting," she says.

"He was trying to share part of his culture with us."

Now you feel sad, too. You don't know Kiran, but you do know what it's like to feel alone.

"Does your mum know you're a werefox?" you ask.

"I don't think so. I only shift at night and sneak out to explore. It's good to have someone else to share my secret with. I suppose for Kiran, being different is like having a secret he doesn't get to share with anyone else. I should be nicer to him."

She turns off the computer and puts away her pencil and paper.

"Right," she says. "Let's clean up the art room so nobody suspects, and then maybe we should write Kiran a note about how beautiful his painting is."

"Yes," you agree. You do like the painting. It is cheerful and fun; just looking at it makes you want to smile.

The two of you write Kiran a note (which you leave in his desk), hang the pictures back up in the corridor, clean up the last of the evidence in the art room, and then slip out of the school and into the night. Pippa wants to race to the cottage, but it isn't fair because her legs are longer, even as a fox cub. She runs circles around you, the keys to the school jangling in her mouth, and together you make your way back home.

Thanks for reading the first adventure of Pippa the Werefox. Her next adventure is *Pippa Parvin and the Mystery of the Missing Pencil.*

ABOUT THE AUTHOR

D.Z. Mah is science fiction and fantasy author, Emily Mah (who also writes contemporary fiction as E.M. Tippetts), and her two young sons. Stuck at home during the 2020 pandemic, they started to get bored and so made up some very silly stories to keep themselves entertained. They hope you are also entertained by the menagerie of mythical creatures and motley crew of characters who brightened their days during a dark time.

Made in the USA
Las Vegas, NV
21 January 2024

84687886R00038